NE...

and the Mystery of the

PINK SPOTS

By Natalia Drakon
Illustrations by Bron Ivy

Nera And The Mystery of The Pink Spots
by Natalia Drakon

First edition.

Text © copyright Natalia Drakon, 2024.
Illustrations © copyright Bron Ivy, 2024.

ISBN 978-1-0685753-0-3

Published by October Dragon Publishing.

Dedication
To Morgan, Arwen and Ruben, my
darling dragons, who inspired this
book with a simple yet magical ask:
"Tell us a story."

Chapter 1.
The Dragons Of
The Mystic Valley

I t is no secret that the dragons of the Mystic Valley are the most beautiful creatures in the whole wide world, maybe even the universe.

These large, majestic dragons are surprisingly light on their feet, moving with unrivalled elegance and agility. They are powerful too, having strong teeth, sharp talons and supple tails that end with a pointy tip like the head of an arrow. For all these reasons, they are excellent hunters and fighters.

Their bodies are covered in vivid, dazzling scales spanning every colour of the rainbow. When they unfurl their huge, formidable wings, they create a spectacular display.

Mystic Valley dragons have beautifully sculptured faces, with elegant narrow snouts. Small horns and bony projections are arranged in different patterns on top of their foreheads like unique crowns.

Their large, mesmerising eyes shine with intelligence and grace but hiding under the surface there is a twinkle of wit and the occasional flicker of good-natured mischief.

There is a saying that if you look into a dragon's eyes, you can never tell a lie.

The dragons are smart, charismatic and sociable, which makes them fiercely protective and loyal friends.

Of all the dragons in the Mystic Valley, Nera stands out as particularly impressive and exceptionally beautiful. Unlike most of the other dragons, who are different, vibrant colours, she is black from the ends of her talons to the tips of her wings.

Nera's unusual, gorgeous, deep black colour makes her shimmer in the sunlight and gleam by the light of the moon. On a cloudy night, or the night of a New Moon, Nera could blend in with the darkness and almost disappear from view.

Nera and the other dragons live cordially in their village in the Mystic Valley, along the Mystic River, only a short flight away from the Mystic Sea.

Their village is made of cosy dens and plenty of open, green spaces where the dragons gather for celebrations, storytelling and performances.

Unless they are hunting or enjoying solo, leisure flights over the nearby lands and oceans, the dragons like nothing better than to be together.

In fact, these dragons are such a friendly bunch that they would happily make up occasions and festivities just to enjoy some roaring fun.

Their lives often feel like an ongoing festival of playing games, dancing, splashing in the river and telling stories together with fire-breathing displays and aerial acrobatics.

There is also plenty of food to go round as each dragon gladly shares their catch with the others.

All in all, the dragons of the Mystic Valley enjoy a good life, filled with joy and laughter.

Then, one morning, everything changed.

Chapter 2.
Pink Spots

That fateful morning Nera could not stop thinking about her friend Joey, who had been away from the village for over a month now. Joey was known to enjoy his lone flights a little bit more than the other dragons. He was an adventurous soul and liked to explore unknown territories.

After discovering some old caves in a nearby mountain range, Joey was on a mission to investigate every last hole, corridor and cavern. "Back in a few days!" Nera remembered him saying. She had a flashback of Joey's giddy snout as he raised his wings and took off.

This was not the first time that he had been missing for days, only to suddenly turn up out of nowhere, all dirty and mucky but happy. Nera loved listening to Joey excitedly recounting where he went and what he saw. But somehow this time felt different. Nera could not shake off a niggling feeling that something was wrong.

Joey returned from the caves that very morning and crash-landed in the middle of the village meeting place. He was breathing heavily and pearly drops of sweat covered his snout and scales. This was a bad sign. Dragons do not sweat unless they are very poorly. The entire village was immediately alerted. All the dragons gathered round Joey trying to figure out what was wrong. Clearly exhausted, Joey just closed his eyes and moaned, not responding to the flurry of questions from the other dragons.

Suddenly, everyone noticed bright pink spots appearing on Joey's vibrant aquatic blue wings. Over the next few days, his

condition worsened until he was completely
covered in pink spots. Every time Joey tried
to spread his wings to fly, the spots itched
terribly and he tossed himself into the river
or rolled on the ground to find some relief.

It was no good. Joey was miserable. He
lost his appetite and good humour. Other
dragons kept bringing him food and water,
and took turns to groom and cuddle him.
But the worst was yet to come.

Over the following days, other dragons
began to develop pink spots on their wings.

Before long, half the dragons in the village were covered in the mysterious pink spots.

Nera was very worried. She spent her days in the library, working tirelessly with Florence, who was the village elder, historian and librarian. Together, they combed through endless old manuscripts, volumes and scrolls.

They found descriptions of foods and conditions that could make dragons unwell. They also found recipes for medicines and remedies that could make dragons well again. Unfortunately, no matter how hard they looked, they couldn't find any mention of pink spots anywhere.

Nera and Florence soon worked out that the pink spots were spread by touch, so they both avoided contact with any dragon who was unwell. Even if it meant coming across as distant and unfriendly — the worst insult for a dragon.

Florence scratched her pearly white head and rubbed her eyes. She strained to remember if she had ever even heard of an illness with pink spots.

"There is nothing in here!" Nera exclaimed, feeling dejected after days of flicking through dusty pages.

Florence sighed. More and more dragons were becoming unwell every day and they still did not know anything about the pink spots. How much worse could this get?

"Right, there is only one thing to do," said Florence. "I must go to the Silver Mountain. There, in the caves within the mountain, lives a wizard troll called Holger. He is an adept healer and knows all about curing rare diseases. And he knows everything there is to know about magical creatures. He is the only one who can help but it won't be easy — he is a right old git. And it's a long way to the Silver Mountain."

Florence gazed towards the horizon and sighed. Heavy silence filled the room until Nera spoke.

"I should go. If things get worse here, you will know what to do better than I would."

Nera had to do all she could to help her fellow dragons. It was the only way.

"Yes, I will go." She was adamant.

Florence narrowed her eyes and studied Nera. Then she nodded.

That evening Nera looked on in desperation as even more dragons developed pink spots and stumbled around the village, dragging their feet and wings and struggling to catch a breath. The spots were becoming itchier, making the affected dragons utterly miserable.

Nobody could sleep. Nobody could rest. Nobody could eat. The sick dragons were growing weaker and weaker.

Nera hated feeling so helpless. The situation was even harder and more heartbreaking because she couldn't even offer her friends a reassuring hug or a consoling nose rub. Knowing she had to hurry, Nera packed some food, water and the directions that Florence had prepared for her.

The next morning, before sunrise, she set off in search of the Silver Mountain.

Chapter 3.
Wizard Troll

For three days and three nights, Nera flew without a break until the Silver Mountain finally appeared on the horizon. She landed at the foot of the mountain by a small lake. Walking slowly into the lake, Nera let the water swallow her whole body. She soaked for a good while and took a long drink. She needed food and more rest but there was no time.

Nera looked up, scanning the mountain's face for the entrance to Holger's cave. Having finally spotted it, she climbed up the mountain and cautiously went inside. A horrible stench hit Nera's nostrils, making her hesitate and stop in her tracks. While dragons are used to strong odours like rotting meat and ageing fish, this was another level of stink. It was like wet, mouldy mulch mixed with decomposing meat, rotting plants and sour milk.

Nera inhaled sharply, hoping to hold her breath for as long as she could to keep out the horrendous smell. She navigated the maze of tunnels wondering if anyone could live here.

Suddenly, she heard a strange, rhythmic noise in the distance. It took Nera a while to work out which direction it was coming from as she made her way through the tunnels. She was getting closer. The smell was getting worse and the noise sounded more and more like snoring. Following the sound, Nera came to a rocky chamber with stalactites hanging from the ceiling and stalagmites sprouting from the floor. Some of them met in the middle and formed curious columns of rock. There were bones and animal parts scattered everywhere and in the far corner there was something resembling a cauldron.

The snoring was coming from the other end of the chamber. Nera could now make out a huge mound of flesh rising and falling with every breath. As she stepped closer, one of the bones on the floor snapped under her paw, sending a crack echoing around the cave. Startled, Nera grumbled quietly. Her voice, bouncing off the cave walls, became amplified until it sounded like a loud, thunderous roar.

The source of the snoring awoke and jumped to its feet. It was a big, tall troll, with broad shoulders and an even broader belly. His face was large, wide and covered in warts while his narrow nose curved like the beak of an owl. The troll's ears stuck out at weird angles, one higher than the other, making his whole head look lopsided. Still groggy from sleeping, the troll rubbed his small eyes and peered blankly at Nera. He had a domineering posture but spoke in a squeaky, high-pitched voice.

"What, where, who?" squeaked the troll, looking around startled. Then his eyes fell on Nera and he gasped, realising that there was a dragon in his cave.

Nera smiled and sat back, trying to look as friendly as possible — which is not always easy for a dragon.

"Hello," she whispered, aware of the acoustics of the rocky room. "Are you Holger? The wizard troll? My name is Nera and I need your help. Please. You see..."

Nera paused because the troll was studying her with a peculiar look in his eyes.

"Yes," he squeaked slowly after a while. "I am Holger, the wizard troll. And you are a dragon! From the Mystic Valley, if I'm not mistaken? Fascinating."

Holger was now closely inspecting Nera. He paced around her in circles, peering at her talons and wings while muttering to himself, clicking his tongue and clapping his hands.

"Magnificent!" he mumbled.

"Ahem," Nera cleared her throat and

continued hesitantly, "It is nice to meet you. I am happy that I found you. Like I was saying, I need your help."

"Yes, there will be time for that," Holger squeaked excitedly, "but first, a little game."

"A game?" Nera gasped. "I don't have time for games. Look, my friends are ill. I need to find help."

"Oh, it is just a little game," squeaked the troll, undeterred. "It won't take long. Listen here, dragon, I have been cooped up alone in this cave for so long that I need a little entertainment. And then we can see what I can do for you. The longer you argue the longer it will take for me to help you. Come on! What say you?"

This was one stubborn troll. Nera lowered her head and sighed.

"Right then," the troll squeaked, rubbing his hands gleefully. "Three riddles. If you guess the answers I will help you."

"And if I don't?" Nera asked, cautiously.

"You will, for sure. I will go easy on you." Holger squeaked and rubbed his chin. "First question: I cannot swim and I cannot fly, but I can still help you cross a river? What am I?"

"You're a bridge." Nera said quickly.

"Yes, very good." Holger clapped excitedly. "Second question: I am a cloud that joins the earth with the sky. What am I?"

Nera thought for a minute. "You are fog," she answered cautiously.

"Yes, yes! Very well!" Holger was hopping gleefully. "Last question! Rain and shine I colour the sky, what am I?"

"A rainbow," Nera said, with audible relief in her voice.

"Yes, yes, yes!" chuckled the troll. "It's true what they say about dragons. You are clever. Now what can I do for you?"

Nera explained that the dragons in her village were falling ill.

"It starts with breathing difficulties and sweats. Then the pink spots appear. The itchy rash covers the wings first, which renders the dragons unable to fly. Then the pink spots spread to the rest of their bodies." Nera finished with a sigh.

Holger snapped his fingers and a large, thick book appeared out of thin air and fell to the ground with a loud thud, raising a cloud of dust. The leather-bound cover read: 'The Book of Potions, Lotions and Other, Useful Concoctions'. The pages of the book were filled with rune-like writing that Nera did not recognise. Holger studied the book for a very long time, humming to himself and slowly turning the large pages. It took so long in fact that Nera, who was exhausted, dozed off.

When she woke up, a fire was crackling under the cauldron, which was filled with a slimy green substance bubbling away. Despite a revolting smell in the air, Nera's tummy rumbled loudly.

"You must be hungry. Come and have some food." Holger stirred the pot of green slime, sending frog's legs and fish eyeballs into a mad whirl.

Nera sniffed the cauldron and grimaced awkwardly. "Um, no thank you."

"Not this, silly," the troll chuckled, "that!" He motioned to another open fire where three huge fish were roasting on a slowly rotating stick.

"OK then, thank you!" Nera hopped over to the fire and swallowed the first fish whole. As she started on the second fish, Holger spoke again.

"The pink spots are caused by a fungal infection. It is a type of mould that can only be found in the deepest of the mountain caves. The dark, damp and stuffy ones."

Nera looked up and around. The dark, damp, stuffy passages of this cave, which she walked through to find Holger, flashed through her mind.

"It is very rare," Holger continued, "but there is a cure. I started working on it with the ingredients I have but I am missing a few and I need you to find them."

Nera nodded as Holger listed what was needed.

"First, you need to go to the Enchanted Forest and find me strands of hair from a unicorn's mane, pixie fairy dust and a handful of leaves and fruits from the golden Loveheart Tree. Now listen carefully. The location of the Loveheart Tree is a secret guarded by the Pixie Fairy Queen herself. You will have to somehow convince her to show you where it is. Good luck."

Holger handed Nera a sack for each of the three ingredients and waved her off. Nera did not move. Holger stared at her, a quizzical look in his eyes.

"I don't know where the Enchanted Forest is," whispered Nera.

Holger sighed and motioned Nera to follow him as he hobbled almost all the way to the cave's exit. He hovered in the shade and shielded his eyes from the sunlight, which showed his green complexion in a rather unflattering light. Then he pointed East.

"It shouldn't take you longer than two days to get there and two days to come back. I expect your return in about a week," he said before hastily turning back inside the cave.

Nera took off once more.

Chapter 4.
Unicorns

Two days later, at dusk, Nera landed in the Enchanted Forest. She crawled under a massive, ancient oak tree and fell fast asleep.

At dawn, Nera was awoken by the birds' morning chorus. She stretched sleepily and looked around in amazement. The forest was beautiful — lush green with tall trees and thick undergrowth. Fallen tree trunks were covered in soft, bright green moss. The rays of sunlight shone through the gaps in the branches and foliage, making the particles of dust and pollen look like they were dancing in the air. Nera felt calm and relaxed as she wandered through the green realm, which was teeming with life. Birds chirped and tweeted. Bees buzzed around aromatic flowers. Beetles and other crawlies scuttled along, busy with their daily chores.

Nera found a lake and enjoyed a nice long soak. The water soothed her scales and filled her with a new sense of joyful hope. She was even happier when she heard a horse-like whinnying nearby. The sound was getting closer. Nera submerged her body in the lake with only her eyes, ears and snout visible above the surface.

"Wonderful," she thought as a family of unicorns approached the edge of the water. Nera stayed still and quiet while watching them drink. She was thinking intently about how best to approach them.

The unicorns were fantastic, magical creatures. The hair that covered their bodies was short and snow white but grew longer down their legs, covering the hooves in a feathering fashion. Their long, silky manes shimmered in the sun while their horns rose proudly in the air like sparkly lances. They communicated using quiet neighs and whinnies and by stroking the ground with their hooves. Nera was mesmerised as she watched their manes floating gently in the breeze.

"I only need a few of those strands of hair," she thought to herself and decided to make a move. Quietly, Nera swam towards the shore. Tiny ripples on the surface of the water were the only sign she was there. She was about halfway across the lake when she lifted her head and emerged from the water. Wanting to keep her distance and avoid spooking the unicorns, Nera stopped and waited for them to notice her.

It did not take long. The unicorns neighed loudly in alarm, reared up on their hind legs and then galloped away, necks stretched forward, legs barely touching the ground.

"No! Wait!" Nera called after them — but the unicorns had already disappeared into the thick forest.

Nera quickly followed the sound of the hooves in the distance. At first, she chased on foot, running through the thick undergrowth of the forest. Then she flew to the top of the forest, jumping and gliding between the crowns of the trees to keep up with the unicorns.

She could only see the occasional glimpse of a shimmering mane or white tail between the trees. The unicorns ran effortlessly through the dense forest stretching endlessly ahead.

"How will I get them to stop?" Nera wondered. "Wait!" she cried out, "I need to talk to you! I won't hurt you!" But her roar came out more forcefully than she intended and spooked the unicorns even more.

The unicorns galloped onto a vast glade with a large ditch filled with muddy water. Without slowing down, most of the unicorns got over the ditch in a single, impressive jump. But one of the younger unicorns didn't make it. Her hoof slipped as she landed on the far side of the ditch. Losing her grip, she tumbled to the bottom of the ditch with a whinny full of fear and panic. She landed awkwardly with a splash, covering her beautiful white coat in mud. Luckily, she wasn't hurt. She pulled herself up just as Nera landed with a swish and peered over the ditch.

On the far side of the ditch, the unicorns stopped and turned around. They whinnied and reared up on their hind legs, clearly trying to get Nera to back off.

"Wait," said Nera, in a calm, hushed voice. "I am not going to hurt you."

The unicorn with the largest horn came to the other edge of the ditch, angrily flaring her nostrils and flattening her ears. "How can we trust you? You are a dragon, the fiercest predator there is!"

"Yes, that I am," Nera admitted proudly, "but right now I need your help and I can also help you."

The young unicorn was still trying to climb the high banks of the ditch, sliding and skidding in the muddy water. Before long, she was exhausted and completely covered in thick sludge.

Nera slowly climbed down to the stranded youngster, ignoring the panicked whinnying of the unicorns pacing nervously on the far side of the ditch. She cautiously approached the young unicorn, asking her to stop struggling before she hurt herself. The unicorn dropped her head and neighed plaintively as Nera drew closer.

"I am going to get you out of here," Nera whispered.

Her soft growl still startled the unicorn and made her shudder. They locked eyes and stared at each other for a while before the unicorn lowered her head again, resigned to her fate.

Nera spread her wings and slowly rose into the air. Hovering over the scared youngster, she gently clasped her huge talons around the unicorn's belly and carefully lifted her out of the ditch. The other unicorns watched with a mix of awe and terror as Nera slowly lowered the young unicorn onto the grass and landed next to her. Nera gave her a gentle nudge with her snout and the unicorn galloped over to rejoin the herd. The unicorns then started to run away again.

"No! Please, I need your help!" Nera called after them, with despair in her voice.

One unicorn stopped at the edge of the forest. She was the one with the largest horn, who had spoken to Nera before. With a watchful eye on the dragon, she waited for her herd to disappear into the safety of the forest. Once the sound of hooves had faded away, she calmly walked back to Nera and introduced herself.

"I am Hippolyta, the Queen Mother of the herd," said the unicorn, her majestic voice commanding respect. "Thank you for saving my daughter."

"You are welcome, Hippolyta. My name is Nera and, as I said, I need your help." Nera quickly told the unicorn Queen about the dire situation back in her village. She explained that she needed just a few strands of hair from a unicorn's mane so Holger could make the potion to cure the poorly dragons.

"Holger?" Hippolyta neighed with laughter, "Well, why didn't you say so? It's good to know that old troll is still around — even though unicorns aren't fond of trolls. And as you just saw, we are petrified of dragons. However, a few strands of hair from my mane are a small price to pay for my daughter's safety. Here, take some." Hippolyta lowered her head.

Nera sliced at the unicorn's shimmering mane with her claw, letting the strands of hair fall into one of the sacks she had brought.

"Thank you," said Nera as she bowed her head. "One more question if I may. Would you know where I can find the forest pixies?"

"Let me guess, Holger needs something from them too?" Hippolyta neighed softly. "You will find them back by the lake. Good luck, dragon."

The unicorn neighed farewell as she galloped away.

Chapter 5.
Pixies

Nera flew back to the lake as the sun was setting and the stars began to appear in the sky. She landed silently behind the thick bushes, which offered shelter and disguise. She had a good view of most of the lake and could observe her surroundings without being noticed.

"Great hideout," thought Nera. Almost immediately she spotted a group of pixies in the distance, frolicking in the moonlit waters. At least, she thought they were pixies.

They were tiny beings, glowing with soft light and each a different colour. The pixies had cute, round faces with large eyes, short hair that shimmered in the moonlight and tiny wings that sparkled silver.

Nera looked on as they splashed in the water, giggling, and dived into the lake using blades of water reeds as a slide. Some would occasionally rest and lounge on the water lilies. As they flicked their wet wings, droplets of water flew in every direction — which made them giggle even more.

The pixies were full of playful mischief. Nera chuckled as she watched one pixie dive under a lily pad, on which some of the others were relaxing, and lift it from underneath so they fell with a splash into the water. This was accompanied by shrieks of delight and more laughter. Nera found the pixies simply adorable and watching them was like a magical dream.

Nera smiled, watching all the fun, and was just about to reveal her presence when she saw a lone pixie standing ashore. Much like Nera, this pixie was watching all the

fun with a dreamy smile but not joining in.
Unlike the other pixies, whose wings
gleamed silver in the moonlight, this pixie
had larger, golden wings and a small,
beautiful crown perched on top of her short
hair.

"The Queen!" gasped Nera.

The Pixie Queen gazed towards the
bushes where Nera was hiding. She
furrowed her little brow, deep in her
thoughts. Then she turned around and
wandered into the forest.

"I must follow," Nera thought. Without making a sound, she blended into the darkness of the night.

Nera became the shadows of the trees as she followed the golden gleam of the queen's wings. The Pixie Queen walked through the forest slowly, majestically, taking in the beauty of the soft shine of the moss, glowing mushrooms and floating lights of the fireflies. The forest was quiet at night but not silent. The constant hum of the night insects was occasionally interrupted by the louder calls of the night birds and the hooting of the owls.

The Queen finally came to a sudden clearing in the thick forest. There, in the middle of the clearing, stood an ancient tree with a golden glow. Its crown, leaves and fruit were all in the shape of a heart. Nera's eyes lit up with excitement.

"Amazing!" she thought, hardly believing her luck.

Holger had told her that the Loveheart Tree was very difficult to find as only the Pixie Queen knew its location. And yet, there it was! As Nera crept forward, eager and excited, she stepped on a twig. It snapped under her paw.

The Queen spun around and shouted "Protect!", raising her arms and unfurling her wings. Nera knew that pose very well. It was the same protective stance dragons assumed when they felt threatened, making themselves look larger and ready to fight whatever came at them.

At the Queen's command, thick roots immediately sprang from the ground while thorny branches descended from the surrounding trees, creating an impenetrable cage around the Loveheart Tree.

"Show yourself! Who are you?" the Queen demanded, peering into the darkness.

Nera stepped out of the shadows, towering over the Pixie Queen.

"Are you a dragon?" asked the Queen, with awe and fear in her eyes. It was the same look that Nera had seen in the unicorns' eyes earlier that day.

"Yes," said Nera, thinking fast about what to say next. Bowing her head, she calmly stated, "My name is Nera. Forgive me for sneaking up on you like this but I need your help."

Once again Nera described the dire situation back in the Mystic Valley where the infectious pink spots were making dragons so unwell. She also told the Queen about Holger brewing a cure.

"So that is why I followed you. I need some pixie dust and a few leaves and pieces of fruit from the magical Loveheart Tree," Nera concluded.

"Hmm, Mystic Valley. I have heard of that place. It is meant to be beautiful," the Queen said thoughtfully. Nera nodded with a smile.

The Queen gently tapped the living cage encasing the tree. "It is all well," she whispered to the branches. As quickly as they had appeared, the roots and thorny branches retreated. The Loveheart Tree glowed intensely.

"I am Norika, the woodland Pixie Queen, and it is my duty to protect this tree. It is very special." Norika wrapped her little arms around the tree trunk affectionately and put her ear to the bark. The branches swayed gently and the leaves rustled in the night breeze. Nera felt an electric sensation that the tree was speaking and the Pixie Queen was listening.

"This is the ancestor tree that started this forest and pumps life into it. This location is secret, passed from Queen to Queen through the generations." Norika looked at Nera with a twinkle in her eye and a half-smile. "And yet here you are, dragon Nera."

"Normally, the forest warns me about intruders and invaders who wish to find the tree. But this time it didn't. Why is that?" Norika stroked the bark of the tree and fluttered to the top branches to have a better look at Nera.

"I don't know," Nera answered honestly. "Perhaps the tree and the forest know that I mean no harm. But I need help, and fast."

"I never had to use the protection spell before so it was interesting to see how it works." Norika nodded. "And I agree with you — the tree knows you mean no harm and has already agreed to help you. Please take what you need. I believe you."

"Thank you," said Nera with relief. She gently collected leaves and fruit from the Loveheart Tree and put them away in one of the sacks that Holger had given her.

"Thank you so much Queen Norika. I will not bother you any longer." Nera bowed her head and was about to take off.

"Didn't you say you also need some pixie dust?" the Queen asked softly.

"The dust!" Nera gasped and nodded, feeling quite embarrassed. "I almost forgot."

"For that we need to go back to the lake. I wonder what my pixies will make of a dragon!" The Queen's laughter sounded like the tinkling of tiny bells as she flew past Nera's face.

Long before they reached the lake, Nera and the Pixie Queen could hear the laughter of the frolicking pixies echoing through the forest. The splashing and sploshing noises grew louder and louder as they got closer to the lake.

When the pixies saw their Queen emerging from the forest they raced to her with bright smiles on their cute faces. However, they stopped mid-flight and gasped in horror at the sight of the dark shape following her. An eerie silence ensued, broken only by the sound of water droplets dripping from the pixies' wings down to the ground. One of the pixies dropped a shiny pebble she was carrying

into the lake and the splash it made
sounded like the loudest of thunders.
Norika laughed gently.

"It's all right, my dear pixies," said
Queen Norika, her voice calm and melodic.
"This is Nera. She is a friendly dragon."

The pixies gasped and cooed collectively.
After only a second or two, a chorus of
joyful, harmonious chatter erupted across
the lake as the pixies swarmed around
Nera. They touched her scales, felt her
wings and inspected her snout and horns.
Nera suddenly found herself surrounded by
the flutter of tiny wings. One pixie
accidentally flew into the dragon's nose,
tickling Nera and causing her to sneeze.

"Achoo!" A ball of fire flared from Nera's
nostrils and left a scorch mark on the
ground.

"Oh, dear, I'm so sorry," whispered Nera,
"Is everyone OK?"

"Wow!" the pixies exclaimed in unison as
they inspected the scorched earth. They
then went back to studying every part of
Nera's body.

Norika beckoned to one of the pixies and whispered in her ear. The little pixie flew up to Nera's face, unclasped a pouch from her belt and offered it to Nera with an adorable smile.

"Bluebell makes fantastic pixie dust," Norika said with a smile. "Now Nera, have a refreshing bath in our lake. The water is wonderfully cool and it will bring back your strength. This is important for you are yet to complete your mission." Norika gazed west, towards the Silver Mountain.

Nera did not need to be invited twice. She walked slowly into the water once more, relishing how cool and soothing it felt against her scales. She let the water wash over her and relaxed, floating in the lake. The pixies continued to fly around her, splashing and thrashing in the lake.

One curious pixie was tracing the triangle at the end of Nera's tail.

"Try this," said Nera, extending her wet tail out of the water to form a slide.

The pixie slid down the dragon's tail with glee, landing in the lake with a splash.

The other pixies all rushed to the end of Nera's tail, giggling and bickering over whose turn it was next. Each pixie had a go sliding down the dragon tail slide, shrieking, screaming and calling for more as they shot out of the water over and over again.

By the time the pixies finally retired to sleep, the moon was fading and the sun was rising over the horizon. Nera felt rested as she took off and flew back to the troll's cave, patting the three sacks containing unicorn hair, Loveheart Tree leaves and fruit, and pixie dust.

"I hope this is all that Holger needs," thought Nera as she once more neared the Silver Mountain.

Chapter 6.
Back And Away Again

"You're back!" Holger squeaked. He eagerly took the items Nera had collected in the Enchanted Forest and added them one by one to the mixture in the cauldron.

The white hair of the unicorn caused the potion to glow with every colour of the rainbow. The leaves from the Loveheart Tree changed it to radiant gold. Bluebell's pixie dust made it sparkle purple. Then the potion bubbled ferociously and turned back to green.

"Wonderful!" Holger squeaked in his high-pitched voice. "Next, you will have to find...". He paused as he squinted at his book of potions.

"Wait!" exclaimed Nera. "I thought you had everything you need now!"

"Shush!" the troll replied, impatiently. "Ah, found it! We will need salt crystals from the plains of Salazar Desert. While you're there, you can also search for a fossil tooth from a prehistoric creature. Bring a sharp one, from a meat eater. And..."

"A prehistoric creature's tooth, like a dinosaur's?" Nera shook her head in disbelief. "You expect me to find a dinosaur's tooth in a desert?! What else? A needle in a haystack, perhaps?"

"Oh, do not fret. It is not as difficult as it sounds, really. In the Salazar Desert there is a large boneyard. It is so huge, actually, that you cannot miss it. In this boneyard lives a flock of vultures. They are vile-looking birds but very useful. They believe that fossils have healing properties so they collect them. Find where they keep them and take one that looks like a tooth. A sharp one, from a meat eater. Easy!"

Holger looked thoughtfully at Nera. "But watch out for their talons. The vultures eat mainly carrion so they have all sorts of dirt on their claws. One scratch and, if they break your skin, or in your case scales, well... let's just say you won't have to worry about the pink spots any more."

"Oh great," muttered Nera.

"You will also need to collect three drops of venom from the emerald scorpion's sting. Yes, that should do it." Holger closed the book with a thud, causing a cloud of dust to rise in the air. He gave Nera two sacks and a glass vial for the venom.

"Before you go, make sure you drink a lot of water and take this fruit." Holger handed Nera a piece of fruit from the Loveheart Tree. "It will quench your thirst and cool you down. At least long enough for you to find and collect everything I need for the potion. Let's hope." Holger stirred the mixture in the cauldron, which bubbled green bubbles and smelled horribly.

"Well off you go!" the troll squeaked, impatiently.

Nera left the cave and took a long drink from the fresh stream flowing outside. Then she looked around. Which way was the Salazar Desert?

"Fly South!" The high-pitched shriek of the troll bounced off the rocks and made Nera's ears ring.

"Thank you!" she roared back, then spread her wings and took off.

Chapter 7.
Heat And Salt

Nera flew for hours. The air became drier and hotter the further south she flew. Eventually, she reached the vast emptiness of the desert. Yellow sand and crumbling rock formations were all she could see stretching to the horizon and beyond.

Nera was hot and tired so she decided to land and find somewhere to rest. The sand was scorching hot. Nera's paws and scales could withstand the immense heat of fire — she was a dragon, after all — but the unrelenting blaze of the sun and dryness of the air made her feel uncomfortable.

As her black scales absorbed more and more heat, for the first time in her life Nera wished she was a different colour. She sighed heavily and took off again, hoping to find some relief in the cooler breeze of the higher air currents.

Nera flew slowly over the sea of sand, her eyes tired from the brightness of the burning sun and the silence broken only by the heavy swish of her own wings. Suddenly, she caught sight of something shiny on the horizon.

"Water? Could this be water?" Nera wondered as she gathered all the strength and energy she had left and flew faster.

Nera soon reached what she had hoped would be a blue lake. Instead, she found only a vast bed of pink and orange salt crystals that gleamed and shimmered in the sunlight, creating a mirage of water. The vast bed of what had once been a sea was now a dried-up, lifeless salt plain. Nera landed with a heavy sigh.

"Well, at least I found the salt," Nera muttered under her hot breath as she scooped some crystals into her sack.

She walked slowly over the cracked ground and rummaged through the layers of salt until she came across some interesting rocks. They were rough and bumpy but with smooth grooves that formed patterns and shapes. Nera could distinguish the outlines of shells and bones. Some of the rocks looked like almost perfect replicas of the creatures captured inside

them. Perhaps these were the creatures
that had lived here millions of years ago.

"Could these be fossils?" Nera wondered.
"None of these look like teeth but they may
come in handy." She studied the peculiar
rocks closely and then put a few different
ones in her sack.

"Right, I really need to find some shade,"
Nera thought. She scanned the hostile
surroundings until she spotted a formation
of rocks and boulders in the distance.
Maybe they could offer some shade as the

sun moved across the sky? Nera flew towards them but as she got closer she realised they were mainly low, wide rocks that cast hardly any shade. She landed behind the largest one, which only just shaded her head.

"This will have to do," Nera sighed, and took a bite out of the Loveheart fruit that Holger had given her. It tasted amazing — the crisp, crunchy and tangy flesh bursting with sweet juice in her mouth. The succulent fruit instantly made her feel cooler and better, and she succumbed to a restful nap.

Chapter 8.
Vultures

When Nera woke up, it was almost sunset. The sun hung low in the sky, turning the horizon vivid orange and pink. Nera heard distant shrieks and squawks above the rocks. Peering from behind a boulder, she saw large birds circling and soaring high in the sky over another set of rocks in the distance.

"Vultures," said Nera, as she smiled and watched the huge birds for a while.

As the sun disappeared behind the horizon, the stars lit up the sky. Darkness descended rapidly, bringing with it the cool, night air. Nera welcomed both.

The darkness and coolness of the desert night made her feel comfortable and confident again. She didn't want to fly and spook the vultures. Taking another bite of the Loveheart fruit, she started running quickly, quietly and effortlessly towards the distant rocks where the vultures had gathered. The smooth sand felt cool under her paws and added a nice bounce to her stride. She also enjoyed the night-time breeze.

Reaching the far rock formation just as the moon rose, Nera saw the boneyard for the first time. Holger was right. It was vast and impossible to miss. Bones gleamed ghostly white in the dim night light. Some were stacked high in neat piles while many more just lay scattered all over the sand.

The vultures wobbled clumsily on their feet as they busied themselves, gathering and organising the bones while also getting ready to sleep. Nera heard them shuffling their feet, fluffing their feathers and whispering in strange raspy voices: "My treasure! Oh, you are so beautiful. You are so magical, so exquisite. My treasure!"

A small group of vultures huddled under the biggest rock in the boneyard. They were busy arranging and rearranging a particular pile of bones that glowed pink and purple in the dark. They looked more like stones than ordinary bones. In fact, they looked similar to the stones that Nera had found earlier. She was convinced that these were the fossils that Holger needed.

Nera melted in with the darkness as she advanced towards the pile of glowing stones. She took care to make each and every step silent but it wasn't easy to navigate the boneyard. Inevitably, she stepped on a bone which cracked under the pressure of her paw. Nera froze. It was only a small crack but the sound bounced off the surrounding rocks, echoing like a dragon-sized boulder dropped from the top of the mountain.

The vultures turned round and quickly formed a line, wings spread wide and touching, sharp beaks and claws at the ready.

"Who's there?!" they screeched together. "Show yourself!"

Then the vultures spotted Nera and, before she could speak, launched their attack.

"Intruder! Attack! Use your claws, use your beaks! Attack! Protect the bones, protect the treasure. Intruder! Burglar! Thief! They want our treasure! Attack!"

The vultures' screeching was loud and piercing. Nera heard wings flapping above her head and claws scraping at her scales. She remembered Holger's clear warning about a vulture's scratch being potentially deadly.

"Stop!" roared Nera, rearing up on her hind legs and spreading her wings. She breathed a circle of fire blazing with high, hot flames and trapping the bones and the vultures inside.

"I am a dragon and will not be called a thief! I am not here to steal your bones but I need your help."

The vultures huddled together again, desperately hopping away from the fire and glaring at Nera with a look of awe and utter terror.

"That's the look," Nera thought to herself with a smirk. She had seen it many times, including just a few days before in the eyes of the unicorns and pixies. Dragons, being the magnificent creatures that they are, inspire reverence and command respect. Nera had to channel this power to protect herself and obtain the fossil tooth.

"Now," Nera growled, blowing smoke out of her nostrils and folding her wings, "I need a fossil tooth, please."

Nera explained the situation back home and how her dragon friends were falling ill with mysterious pink spots. She talked about Holger brewing the cure and the missing ingredients, one of which is a fossil tooth from an ancient creature.

The vultures squawked and screeched among themselves, clearly unsure of what to do about a huge, fire-breathing creature in the middle of their boneyard.

An old, ragged-looking vulture stared hard at Nera, turning and tilting his head sideways to give both of his eyes a good, long goggle.

"No! You are not a dragon!" he finally screeched with great conviction. "We've heard of dragons. Dragons are not thieves."

The other vultures erupted in a chorus of agreement.

"No, I am not a thief but yes, I am a dragon," said Nera flabbergasted, shaking then nodding her head.

"But you want to steal one of our fossils so you are a thief and not a dragon," said the old vulture, looking at Nera suspiciously.

"Wait... what?!" replied Nera, feeling confused and exasperated. "Have you listened to anything that I've just told you? I don't want to steal a fossil tooth. I hope you will give me one to help me and my village. Please?"

"No, no, no," replied the old vulture, shaking his head.

The chorus of vultures behind him all echoed his refusal, screeching, "No, no, no!"

"We do not give away our treasure. If you want it, you will have to take it or steal it. So, you are a thief and not a dragon."

"Thief yes, dragon no! Thief yes, dragon no!" chanted all the vultures, nodding their heads vehemently.

"Stop!" exclaimed Nera. She blew a fire ball into the fire circle, which flared up into the sky with renewed intensity.

"If I wanted to just take the fossil tooth I would have done it by now, along with a few roasted vultures," she said fiercely, and looked at the birds with hungry eyes.

The vultures huddled more closely together and used their wings to shield themselves. The old vulture looked for a way to escape as Nera crept closer to him but the wall of fire was burning high.

"And yet, I am talking to you instead," said Nera, slowly. An idea popped into her head. "But, of course, I can see how you might think I want to take your fossils. And you are right, dragons don't steal. I am a dragon, therefore not a thief. Besides, you are doing a great job of protecting your treasure."

"Really?" replied the chorus of vultures, slightly taken aback by this unexpected compliment. "We mean... yes we are!"

They exchanged puzzled looks. The old vulture, enjoying Nera's praise, puffed up his chest and fluffed up his wing feathers.

"Of course," Nera continued, contemplating the power of flattery, "and I would do the same. I can see you value your treasure so I have a suggestion."

From her sack, Nera took out the fossil rocks she had collected from the salt plains. She looked with amazement as they glowed bright orange.

"How about a trade?" she offered.

The vultures' eyes lit up and their beaks hung open. "Beautiful!" said one. "Amazing!" said another. "Magical!" "Precious!" echoed the others.

"Now," asked Nera, "do you have a fossil tooth? A sharp one, from an ancient meat eater, that you would be willing to trade?"

The vultures huddled together, squawking and screeching, until one little vulture hobbled over to the treasure pit and started to rummage around. Nera waited patiently. The old vulture continued to peer at the glowing, orange fossils she had brought along.

Eventually, the little vulture hobbled back with a selection of large, curved, fossilised teeth. Some of these teeth had smooth edges. Others had jagged edges and, despite being embedded in rock and buried for millions of years, they still looked sharp.

They also glowed purple. The little vulture looked on as the old vulture picked one rather small tooth and handed it to Nera.

"Here you go," said the old vulture. He then used his wings to start gathering all of Nera's fossils from the salt plains towards himself.

"What are you doing?!" asked Nera indignantly, puffing smoke out her nostrils. "The trade is one-for-one. And I would like to choose for myself." She selected a large, curved tooth with jagged edges. "I'll take this one. Now pick one of my fossils."

"No, no, no!" protested the old vulture, while the others all shook their heads vigorously in support. "For that tooth, we'll have to take all your fossils!"

"Oh no you won't!" exclaimed Nera. "How is that fair? No way." She decided to haggle. "You can have two."

The vultures huddled together to consider the offer, flapping their wings, muttering and hopping over each other.

"For the big tooth... two fossils or no deal!" they eventually screeched.

"Fine!" replied Nera, with a smirk. The old vulture picked out two fossils he liked.

"You drive a hard bargain," said Nera, placing the fossil tooth in her sack together with the rest of her fossils.

The fire circle was dying down by now. The vultures nestled together over their treasure pit, inspecting and admiring the two new additions to their fossil collection.

The whispers of 'treasure', 'precious' and 'magical' slowly faded away as the vultures slumbered in a huddle.

Nera smiled and took off.

Chapter 9.
The Emerald Scorpion

Nera flew through the night, scanning the desert below that was shrouded in darkness. "Next, the emerald scorpion. How do I find it?" she wondered.

That's when she noticed a little green light that was moving about, scuttling over the sand and rocks. Could that be it? Nera swerved and landed quietly on the sand. Sure enough, she spotted a large creature with eight legs, chunky pincers and a sting hanging from the tip of a curled tail. The creature was glowing bright green. Emerald green. The scorpion was sitting on a rock, panting when Nera approached it.

"Hello, are you the emerald scorpion?" asked Nera, wanting to be sure that she had identified the creature correctly.

"Don't care," replied the scorpion and began scuttling away.

"Wait, I need your help!" Nera followed the scorpion.

"Don't care. Will you be quiet? I'm hungry and I'm trying to hunt. Shush!" said the scorpion, brashly.

"How rude," thought Nera, but remained silent. Being a dragon and hence a skilful hunter, she knew that hunting requires extreme focus and determination. She would hate any distractions while she was hunting.

Nera therefore sat back, folded her wings and watched silently as the scorpion tried to catch beetles, dragonflies and even a small mouse and a lizard. She marvelled at the way the desert came alive at night, many creatures emerging during the cool, night hours to avoid the scorching days.

Meanwhile the scorpion failed miserably every time he tried to catch something.

"You're not very good at hunting," said Nera eventually, with a note of surprise and disappointment in her voice.

"How dare you!?" the scorpion gasped. "I am a formidable hunter! You should have seen me when I was younger. I could catch a mouse and a lizard every night. I was so fast I could even catch a bird!" The scorpion snapped his pincers at the air pretending to catch his prey. "But I am old now," the scorpion sighed. "My senses are not the same and neither is my speed."

"Well, listen," replied Nera, "I need three drops of your venom to help my friends get better." She quickly explained the situation back home: the dragons were ill with the mysterious pink spots and Holger was working on the cure.

"You are not listening!" the scorpion grumbled. "I don't care!"

"Are you grumpy because you're hungry or is that an age thing too?!" Nera was losing patience with the scorpion.

His venom was the final thing she needed and she wanted to get away from the desert as soon as possible.

"How rude!" started the scorpion.

Nera cut him off. "Look, I'm in a hurry. I was going to help you by catching dinner for you in exchange for three drops of your venom. But, given your age, maybe your venom is also no longer effective so I'm off to find another emerald scorpion. Bye!"

"Wait!" said the scorpion, hastily. "You're willing to catch something for me?"

"Yes, that is my offer," said Nera. "But how do I know if your venom is any good?"

"Why don't you come closer and find out?" asked the scorpion, maliciously. He glared at Nera as he shook his tail with a droplet of venom glistening at the tip. Nera held his stare and he finally snapped his pincers.

"But for three drops of my venom you will have to bring me three dinners," insisted the scorpion.

"Fine!" Nera ran off into the night.

She was back in no time with a mouse, a lizard and a large centipede. The scorpion snapped his pincers excitedly. Nera approached him with her glass vial at the ready and he squeezed three drops of his venom into it. Nera looked on with interest as the bright green venom sizzled and swirled inside the vial.

"Thank you," she said, sighing with relief.

Chapter 10.
Away Once More

Nera lay down on a patch of cool sand and finished the Loveheart fruit. Before sunrise, while it was still cool, she began her long flight back to Holger's cave. She was utterly exhausted by the time she landed at the cave's entrance. Crawling inside, she gave the troll the three items he had asked for: the salt crystals, fossil tooth and drops of venom.

"Excellent", Holger squeaked. He promptly took the ingredients from the desert and arranged them next to the cauldron, where the mixture was bubbling away. He took out a pestle and mortar and proceeded to vigorously grind the salt crystals.

Meanwhile, Nera unceremoniously helped herself to some rabbits that Holger had left roasting over the fire.

"Holger?" she asked, chewing on a rabbit's leg so that crunching sounds echoed around the cave.

"Hmm?" replied the troll, huffing and puffing as he strained to turn the crystals into the finest of powders.

"Can you tell me more about the fossils? What are they and why do they glow in the dark?"

"Do they now?" Holger paused and looked at her excitedly. "Fantastic! This is better than I thought. Fossils are the bones and shells of creatures that lived thousands or even millions of years ago. When these creatures died, their flesh was either eaten or just rotted away, leaving only the skeleton behind — which would normally have turned to dust by now."

Holger raised his voice as he resumed
pounding the salt crystals. "But, if the
skeleton gets covered by earth or mud and
cut off from the air, then over many years
rock can form around it and preserve it.
These fossils, as we call them, can become
coated with other minerals, some of which
glow in the dark."

"Cool," said Nera, "but why do they glow
with different colours?"

"What do you mean?" Holger stopped
grinding the crystals.

"Well, the tooth glowed pink, or more a sort of purple, when I first saw it at night," explained Nera. "But the shell fossils I collected glow orange."

"The colour is determined by the other minerals present in the fossil and the surrounding rock." Holger set down the bowl of salt powder and rubbed his hands together. "Can I see one of your fossils, please?"

Nera passed him one of the fossils which he inspected with a magnifying glass.

"This is beautiful. It's the shell of a sea creature that lived millions of years before us. How magnificent!" Holger commented with great interest.

"You can keep this one as well, if you like." Nera offered. "I have a couple more to show back home."

"Thank you," replied the troll, quickly stashing the fossil away. "Now back to work."

Holger was finally happy with how finely the salt crystals were ground and tipped them into the cauldron. A thick, fizzing foam formed over the top of the mixture. He then threw in the fossil tooth, resulting in a puff of pink smoke. Finally, he added the drops of scorpion's venom, causing a small explosion to echo around the cave. Holger and Nera coughed on the green smoke that engulfed them.

"Is it supposed to help me or kill me?" Nera croaked, shaking her head.

"Nonsense!" squeaked Holger through fits of coughing, his eyes streaming with tears. "It is just as it's meant to be, brewing nicely. Now for the final ingredients."

"What?!" exclaimed Nera. "You need more stuff?"

"Yes, yes" Holger nodded. "I have not been out for years and my pantry is almost empty! Also, this is not an easy recipe, I'll have you know." He paused and buried his nose in the potion book.

"Ah yes, here it is. To finish it off, we need seahorse bubbles, scales from a mermaid's tail and..." Holger squinted at the book and muttered under his breath. "Yes, a black pearl! A black pearl is required." He concluded. "You need to go to the Azure Sea where you'll find all these things. Go now! The sooner you go, the sooner you'll be back."

"Um... seahorse bubbles?" Nera looked at Holger quizzically.

"Yes, seahorse bubbles! You see, seahorses like to dance. When the dance is going particularly well, they blow bubbles. Now, these are not just any bubbles. They are special, happy bubbles. These bubbles have a pulsating, glowing surface that makes them more like orbs, really, and they linger in the water for a few days. Once you collect them, you must hurry to bring them back or else they will pop."

Holger explained all this quickly while ushering Nera out of his cave. "Go now! Go, go, go!"

"Right," sighed Nera and left.

Chapter 11.
Underwater Show

Nera wasn't happy to be sent on another journey but at least she was going to the sea. Dragons love the sea — the waves, the saltiness, the creatures living in it. They can hold their breath under water for a very long time, up to an hour, almost like turtles.

Nera was also curious about meeting the mermaids. Although still tired and worried about her friends, Nera could not help but smile with excitement as she spread her wings and took to the skies once more.

She could smell the sea in the air before it came into view. The vast surface of the water shimmered in the sun and rippled with small waves. The blue was so inviting that Nera giggled with joy as she flew low, skimming the surface of the water with her talons. Suddenly, she shot up high in the air and, with a joyful roar, let her body fall in a straight line all the way down, entering the sea like an arrow.

The water felt like soft silk on her scales, wrapping her entire body in a safe, blissful coolness. She sank deeper and deeper, the water slowing her down, giving her time to take in the beauty of the underwater world — so different from her own and utterly unique. It appeared serene at first, hiding realms of busy, bustling life under the impression of calm and quiet.

Nera swam effortlessly along, in awe of the underwater plants, coral reefs and wonderful creatures lurking in every crevice, hole and gap. She felt like she could stay in this underwater paradise forever, only resurfacing to catch a breath.

But the mission was clear in her head: find the seahorses.

All the same, she enjoyed every moment of swimming past various creatures and admiring the vivid colours and curious shapes and sizes of underwater life. She dived into a dark cave where she bumped into a huge shark. He showed off his teeth in a challenging display.

"Oh, really?" Nera giggled, and grinned broadly at the shark to show off her own razor-sharp teeth. The shark promptly swam away and disappeared into the deep blue. At that moment, Nera sensed a commotion outside the cave.

"Mermaids!" she gasped, as the gorgeous, half-human, half-fish creatures rushed past.

The mermaids were chattering among themselves. "Come on, hurry up, the show is about start! Faster, faster, we don't want to be late! We don't want miss a thing!"

A cuttlefish drifted by the cave's opening. Nera stuck out her snout to nudge her. "Hey, where are the mermaids going?" she asked.

The cuttlefish, taken by surprise, started pulsating vividly, sending waves of colour down her body, arms and tentacles. She was unsure yet curious about the creature that was talking to her.

"Can you talk?" asked Nera, her calm voice floating out of the cave. "Can you tell me where they are going?"

The cuttlefish replied slowly and quietly, stressing every word. "The seahorse dance show. By the coral tower over there." She pointed by extending all her arms into the shape of an arrow.

"Thanks," said Nera as she emerged from the cave to get a better look. The cuttlefish once again began pulsating madly at the sight of a dragon and promptly swam away.

Nera followed the mermaids, keeping her distance. As she approached the coral tower, she hid behind a giant kelp forest. The seaweed swayed gently with the current, looking like a curtain about to be parted for a show. Peering through the plants, Nera saw the mermaids perched on rocks and intently watching swarms of seahorses.

There were thousands of the little creatures everywhere, gathered over a red coral reef bed. They resembled tiny horse heads and necks floating upright with elaborate fins on their backs and chunky, coiled tails. As these alien-looking seahorses bobbed gently up and down in the water, they gleamed and shimmered with many different colours. Their fins floated gracefully and they used their horse-like snouts to greet each other.

Suddenly, as if music began to play that only they could hear, the seahorses started to dance. They turned and twirled, flipped and somersaulted, twisted and swayed, creating complex figures and formations. It was a mesmerising spectacle and Nera could see why the mermaids had been so keen not to miss it. The audience was entranced by the seahorses' fascinating display. Nera watched as they paired up and waltzed off the coral dance floor together.

Nera gasped as she suddenly realised what was happening. "They are looking for a mate!" she said to herself. "This is a mating dance!"

Then she remembered what she had come to collect. "But where are the bubbles? Why are they not blowing any bubbles?!"

Nera started to worry. "I need to think of something, and fast." After all, she had no idea how long this mating display was going to last. Then she had a thought.

"I shouldn't, I wouldn't, I couldn't... or could I?" Nera whispered slyly to herself.

Nera had realised that in some ways seahorses were similar to dragons — slender snouts, curled up tails, fins flailing a bit like wings. There was a huge difference in size, of course, but the seahorses seemed to be in a kind of dance trance and might not notice.

Without thinking further in case she changed her mind, Nera allowed the water to guide her movements as she left the shelter of the kelp forest and gently floated among the seahorses. She raised her chin,

folded her wings back and curled up her tail as much as she could. Despite the massive difference in size, the seahorses didn't seem to notice that there was a dragon swimming among them. As if entranced, they simply continued with their own dance routine.

Nera started to dance, swaying slowly from side to side, twirling and flipping while gently curling and uncurling her tail. She ignored the gasps from the mermaids and the rest of the audience, as well as all the fingers and fins pointing at her. Still very conscious of her size, Nera slowed down her every move to look even more graceful and elegant. She relaxed and let herself enjoy the gentle dancing.

Then it was time to put her plan into action. She blew a flurry of bubbles out of her snout, hoping that the seahorses would start blowing bubbles as well. In response, the seahorses went crazy. They started to dance faster, chasing Nera's bubbles in a frenzy of quick, jerky movements, flips and spins.

All of a sudden, a beautiful, crimson-red seahorse swam towards Nera and started blowing wonderful, vivid red bubbles. The other seahorses started blowing bubbles too, each producing a different colour, until the shimmering, pulsating bubbles lit up the deep blue water like fireworks. Just like Holger had said, the bubbles did not burst but lingered in the water like bright orbs. Nera collected a few in her pouch.

"Thank you," thought Nera with a smile, and slowly floated off the coral dance floor into the audience of mermaids.

The mermaids immediately swarmed around Nera, laughing and tickling her with their beautiful swishy tails.

"Hello Dragon!" cheered the mermaids. "You are a fabulous dancer! So beautiful. So wonderful! So grand!"

Nera floated slowly to the surface, like the centrepiece of a mermaid carousel, and took a deep breath.

"It worked!" she exclaimed with relief.

Then, Nera took a moment to study the beautiful mermaids who surfaced with her. Each of them had long hair in a distinctive shade of green and blue that matched the colour of their large eyes and full lips. They were happy and energetic creatures, constantly smiling, laughing and giggling. Their tails shimmered and gleamed with different colours arranged in vibrant marble patterns. The mermaids happily flicked their tails over the waves so the scales reflected the sunlight. The effect was stunning.

Once more, Nera recounted the events in her village and the reason she came to the sea. She explained that Holger needed mermaid scales for the potion and asked politely if she could have some. The mermaids laughed and told Nera they shed scales all the time to keep their tails shiny and bright. Nera soon had a pouch full of the mermaid scales she needed.

Chapter 12.
The Last Ingredient

"The last thing Holger needs to complete the potion is a black pearl," explained Nera. "Where can I find one, please?"

The mermaids swarmed around Nera, all chattering at once to answer her question. "Under the sea, buried at the bottom. You have to find clams. Most have white shells. They have white pearls inside. But some have dark bands around the edges. Like a black border. Those contain the black pearls."

Suddenly it went quiet as all the mermaids dived down to the sea bed. Nera watched in amazement as the mermaids took the search upon themselves, combing the sand with their hands, looking under every rock, picking up clams and inspecting them. They shook the clams vigorously, listening for rattling sounds within.

Finally, a small, bright green mermaid shot from behind an underwater rock all the way to the surface. This young mermaid was clutching a clam with a black band, which she excitedly passed to Nera. She pried it open with her claw to find a beautiful, iridescent black pearl inside. It was perfect.

"Thank you so much!" Nera exclaimed. The little mermaid smiled shyly and swam away. Other mermaids huddled around Nera to admire the pearl.

"It is so beautiful!" they cried with delight. "One of the best we have ever seen! Well done Mara!" They cheered the little girl mermaid, who quickly disappeared back into the sea.

"Mara is very shy," the mermaids explained, "and doesn't talk much. But she's the best seeker and finder if you're looking for something." They laughed delightfully.

"Thank you ever so much for all your help and I hope to see you again sometime," said Nera with a smile.

She then spread her wings and took off. She barrelled through the air to shake the last drops of water from her body and then, with a flick of her powerful wings, turned towards the Silver Mountain.

The mermaids cheered and waved long after the dragon disappeared beyond the horizon.

* * *

Back at the cave, Holger carefully added the seahorse bubbles, the mermaid scales and the black pearl to the mixture in the cauldron. The potion fizzed, hissed and bubbled violently and gave off a thick, black cloud of smoke.

When the smoke finally settled on the surface of the mixture, Holger fished out the fossil tooth and the black pearl. At that very moment, with a loud puff, the potion froze turning into a block of light green jelly containing deep green swirls.

"Yes, this is it!" Holger rubbed his hands together "It's finished!"

"At last!" Nera sighed with relief. "What about the fossil tooth and the black pearl?"

"Ah yes, this is really good!" Holger squeaked excitedly. "These two things are so hardy and powerful they only need to stew with the brew and then I can reuse them in other potions. They're sort of a payment for my service," Holger chuckled. "I put a lot of stuff from my stash into this potion, not to mention my time, knowledge and skills."

Holger wiped the tooth and the pearl and carefully wrapped them in separate pieces of cloth before putting them away in a wooden chest. He then busied himself tidying away the other potion ingredients.

"That's fair and I am very grateful," said Nera thoughtfully.

"You're welcome," said Holger, "but let's make sure it definitely worked." He pulled out an old twisted twig from his pocket.

"What's that?" asked Nera.

"Why, my wand of course," Holger chuckled and proceeded to cast a spell.

"Up, up, up there goes the block,
Down, down, down here marbles flock."

Nera watched in amazement as the block of jelly rose from the cauldron and floated in the air. As Holger finished the spell, the block turned into hundreds of small, green jelly marbles that neatly filled a jar he had set on the cave's floor.

"Perfect!" squeaked Holger. He picked one jelly marble out of the jar and studied it by the light of the fire. "Yes, this should do. Now open wide." He turned to Nera.

"What?" Nera sounded alarmed. "Nah," she shook her head, "I do not have any pink spots so I don't have to take it, thank you very much."

"This will protect you from getting sick, but suit yourself," Holger sighed. "Of course, by now all your village is most likely infected so you'll be flying into a highly contagious area. You will have to get very close to the sick dragons to give them the medicine. The chances of you getting sick are pretty high, I'd say."

Nera did not have to think long about how unwell dragons were once they developed the pink spots.

"Oh, give it here!" said Nera. She swallowed the marble and grimaced.

"Ugh, disgusting!" she moaned, trying not to gag as the jelly exploded in her mouth, tasting like sickly sweet, rotten eggs.

"Yes, yes, yes" Holger muttered. "What do you expect medicine to taste like, hmm? Most importantly, it will help you and your village. Anyway, you need to be going. Here are the dosage instructions." Holger rolled up a little parchment and attached it to the jar with a ribbon.

"Thank you, Holger." Nera bowed her head and left.

Chapter 13.
Return To The
Mystic Valley

Nera flew back to the Mystic Valley with a heavy feeling in her heart, worrying what she would find back at the village. Sure enough, things were bad.

As Holger had predicted, all the dragons were now covered in pink spots, scratching and restless. Some were so exhausted that they just lay motionless on the ground. They looked thin and pale under the weight of the pink spots.

"Oh no! There is no time to lose. I must be quick!" thought Nera, and set to work.

She gave each and every dragon a marble of medicine, hoping with all her heart that it was not too late. The dragons were so poorly that none protested the vile taste of the marble.

Only when the job was done, and all the dragons had received their first dose of the medicine, did Nera finally crawl into her den. Exhausted, but also overwhelmingly happy to be home, she soon fell into a deep and restful sleep.

When she woke the next morning, she still felt groggy and sleepy. Nevertheless, she dutifully got up to give the dragons their second dose of the medicine.

She repeated this routine for two more days until, on the third morning, Nera woke up to find her village was rid of the spots!

The dragons were feeling much better and perking up fast. Within a week, the hustle and bustle of the village had returned. Nera could not have felt happier to witness this rapid recovery.

The village was buzzing with excitement as preparations for a big party were under way. What better way to celebrate the full recuperation of each and every dragon?

When it came, the day of the party was beautiful and sunny. The celebrations started with the dragon elders giving a speech to thank and honour Nera.

"This is a very special celebration! We give thanks for the return of our health and to Nera, our superhero dragon, whose courage and loyalty made it happen! Thank you, Nera, for bringing us the cure!"

Florence, the librarian and elder, hugged Nera while all the dragons cheered, whooped and roared in unison.

Joey, the first dragon who had fallen ill, now stood strong and tall among the crowd. When Nera glanced in his direction, he gave her a nod and a beaming smile. She grinned back at him.

For the next however many days — no one can remember the exact number — the dragons feasted, danced, sang, breathed fire displays and then feasted some more.

Nera retold her adventures over and over again as the dragons listened intently,

asked questions and cheered every step of the story. They hugged, rubbed noses and thanked Nera over and over again, presenting her with the nicest and juiciest fish as well as lovely lemon curd cheese and honey.

"Hmm, my favourite!" Nera licked her face and took a moment, saying her own silent grace, before rejoicing with the other dragons.

THE END

Author's Thanks

Thanks to Dave for honest and constructive feedback that always challenges me to do better; as well as support and encouragement to see my projects through.

Thanks to Bron Ivy for magical and unique illustrations, which brought Nera to life for everyone to enjoy.

Thanks to Ian Rowland for reviewing the text, taking care of the page layout, digitally editing the illustrations and guiding me through the self-publishing process.

Printed in Dunstable, United Kingdom